AVENGERS K #1
AVENGERS VS. ULTRON

JIM ZUB
SCRIPT

WOO BIN CHOI with JAE SUNG LEE, MIN JU LEE, JAE WOONG LEE, HEE YE CHO, JI HEE CHOI, and IN YOUNG LEE
ART

VC's CORY PETIT
LETTERS

WOO BIN CHOI WITH **JAE SUNG LEE** and **MYOUNG HUI LEE**
COVER ART

WOO CHUL LEE
VARIANT COVER ART

AVENGERS VS. ULTRON is adapted from *AGE OF ULTRON #10AI*;
AVENGERS ORIGINS: VISION (2012) #1; and *AVENGERS (1963) #57, #67*, and *#161-162*.
Adaptations written by SI YEON PARK and translated by JI EUN PARK

AVENGERS created by STAN LEE and JACK KIRBY

Original comics written by MARK WAID, KYLE HIGGINS, ALEC SIEGEL, ROY THOMAS, and JIM SHOOTER;
d illustrated by ANDRÉ LIMA ARAÚJO, STÉPHANE PERGER, JOHN BUSCEMA, BARRY WINDSOR-SMITH, and GEORGE PÉREZ

Editor SARAH BRUNSTAD
Manager, Licensed Publishing JEFF REINGOLD
VP, Brand Management & Development, Asia C.B. CEBULSKI
VP, Production & Special Projects JEFF YOUNGQUIST
SVP Print, Sales & Marketing DAVID GABRIEL
Associate Manager, Digital Assets JOE HOCHSTEIN
Associate Managing Editor ALEX STARBUCK
Editors, Special Projects JENNIFER GRÜNWALD & MARK D. BEAZLEY
Book Designer: ADAM DEL RE

Editor In Chief AXEL ALONSO
Chief Creative Officer JOE QUESADA
Publisher DAN BUCKLEY
Executive Producer ALAN FINE

ABDO
Spotlight

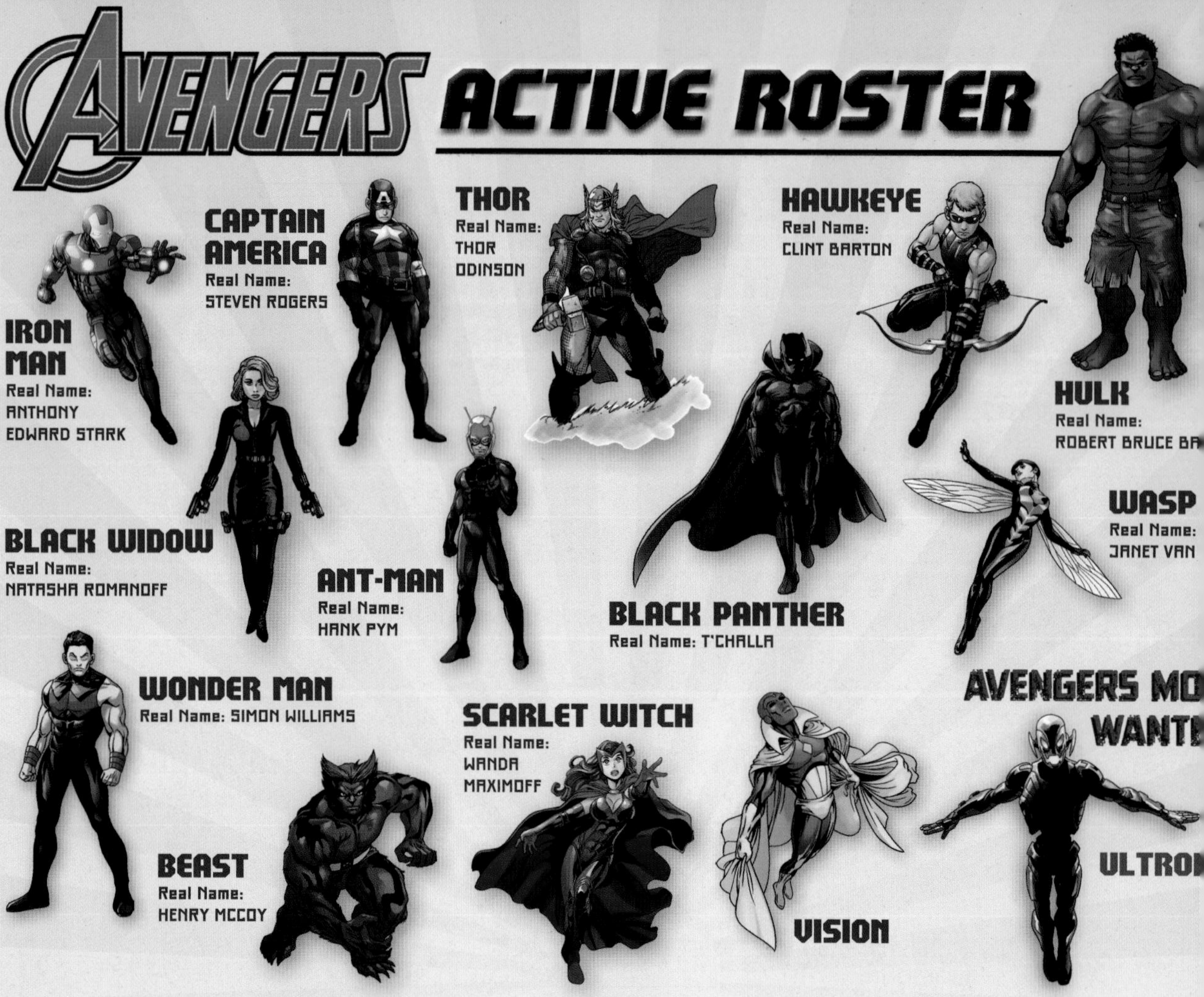
AVENGERS
ACTIVE ROSTER
IRON MAN
Real Name:
ANTHONY EDWARD STARK
CAPTAIN AMERICA
Real Name:
STEVEN ROGERS
THOR
Real Name:
THOR ODINSON
HAWKEYE
Real Name:
CLINT BARTON
HULK
Real Name:
ROBERT BRUCE BA
BLACK WIDOW
Real Name:
NATASHA ROMANOFF
ANT-MAN
Real Name:
HANK PYM
BLACK PANTHER
Real Name: T'CHALLA
WASP
Real Name:
JANET VAN
WONDER MAN
Real Name: SIMON WILLIAMS
SCARLET WITCH
Real Name:
WANDA MAXIMOFF
AVENGERS MO
WANT
BEAST
Real Name:
HENRY MCCOY
VISION
ULTRO

ABDOPUBLISHING.COM

Reinforced library bound edition published in 2017 by Spotlight, a division of ABDO, PO Box 398166, Minneapolis, Minnesota 55439.
Spotlight produces high-quality reinforced library bound editions for schools and libraries. Published by agreement with Marvel Characters, Inc.
Printed in the United States of America, North Mankato, Minnesota.

092016 012017

MARVEL
marvelkids.com

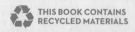

THIS BOOK CONTAINS RECYCLED MATERIALS

PUBLISHER'S CATALOGING IN PUBLICATION DATA

Names: Zub, Jim, author. | Choi, Woo Bin ; Lee, Jae Sung ; Lee, Min Ju; Lee, Jae Woong ; Cho, Hee Ye ; Choi, Ji Hee ; Lee, In Young, illustrators.
Title: Avengers vs. Ultron / writer: Jim Zub ; art: Woo Bin Choi ; Jae Sung Lee ; Min Ju Lee ; Jae Woong Lee, Hee Ye Cho, Ji Hee Choi, In Young Lee
Description: Reinforced library bound edition. | Minneapolis, Minnesota : Spotlight, 2017. | Series: Avengers K
Summary: Ant-Man, Iron Man, Captain America, Thor, Hawkeye, and other fan-favorite Avengers take on Ultron as he plots to destroy the world.
Identifiers: LCCN 2016941682 | ISBN 9781614795681 (v.1 ; lib. bdg.) | ISBN 9781614795698 (v.2 ; lib. bdg.) | ISBN 9781614795704 (v.3 ; lib. bdg.) | ISBN 9781614795711 (v.4 ; lib. bdg.) | ISBN 9781614795728 (v.5 ; lib. bdg.) | ISBN 9781614795735 (v.6 ; lib. bdg.)
Subjects: LCSH: Avengers (Fictitious characters)--Juvenile fiction. | Super heroes--Juvenile fiction. | Comic books, strips, etc.--Juvenile fiction. | Graphic novels--Juvenile fiction.
Classification: DDC 741.5--dc23
LC record available at https://lccn.loc.gov/2016941682

ABDO
Spotlight

A Division of ABDO
abdopublishing.com

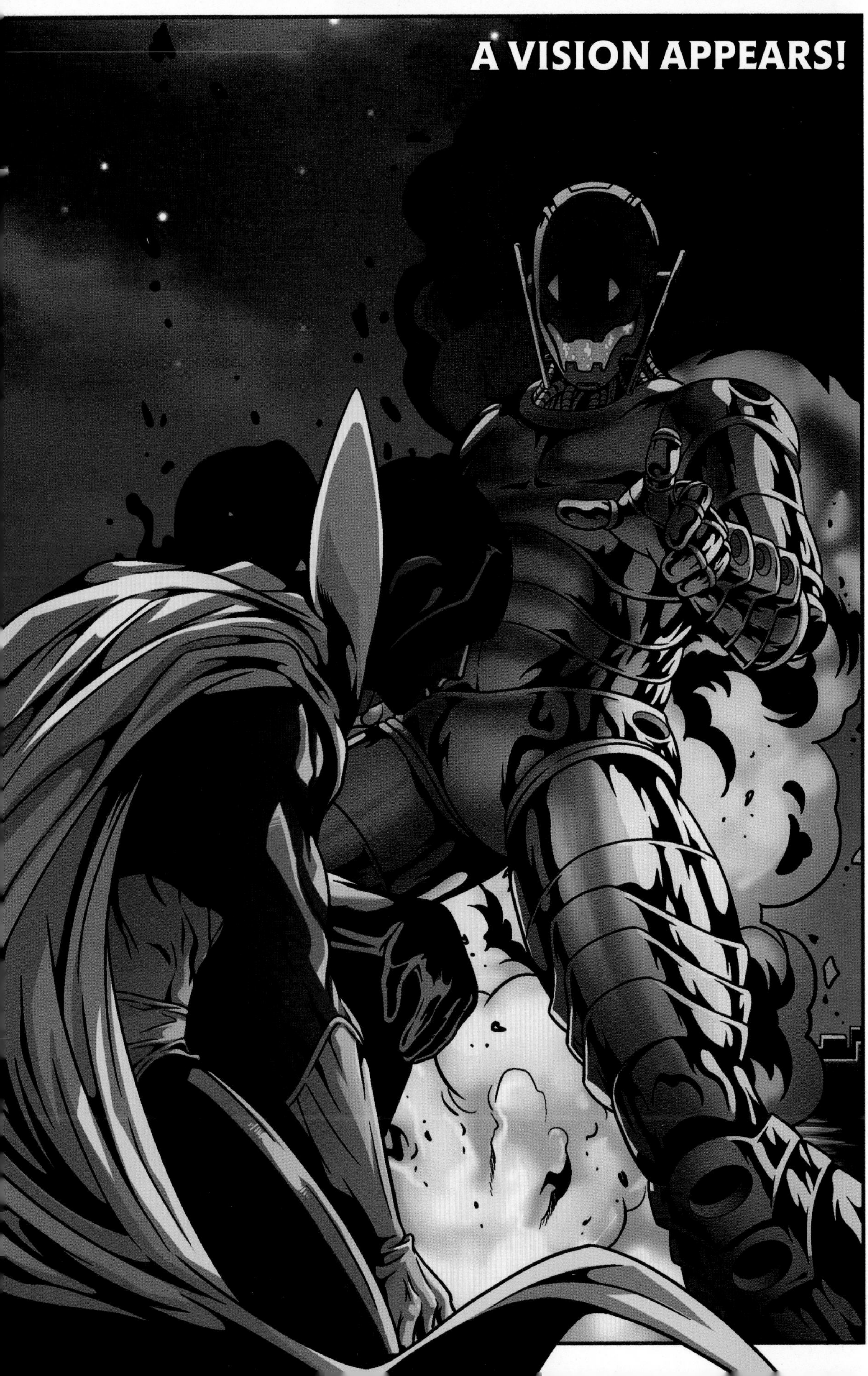
A VISION APPEARS!

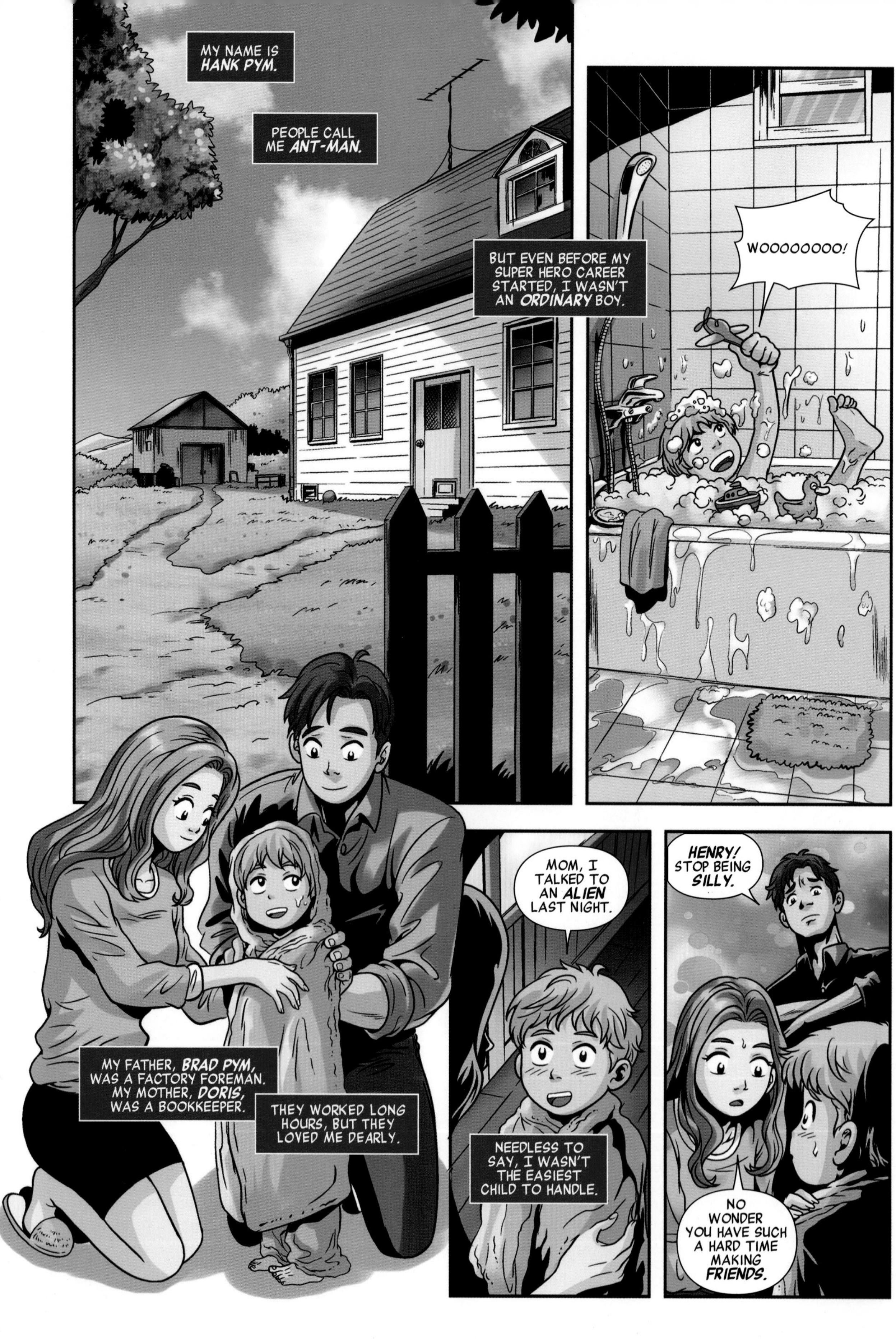
MY NAME IS HANK PYM.
PEOPLE CALL ME ANT-MAN.
BUT EVEN BEFORE MY SUPER HERO CAREER STARTED, I WASN'T AN ORDINARY BOY.
WOOOOOOOO!
MY FATHER, BRAD PYM, WAS A FACTORY FOREMAN. MY MOTHER, DORIS, WAS A BOOKKEEPER.
THEY WORKED LONG HOURS, BUT THEY LOVED ME DEARLY.
MOM, I TALKED TO AN ALIEN LAST NIGHT.
NEEDLESS TO SAY, I WASN'T THE EASIEST CHILD TO HANDLE.
HENRY! STOP BEING SILLY.
NO WONDER YOU HAVE SUCH A HARD TIME MAKING FRIENDS.

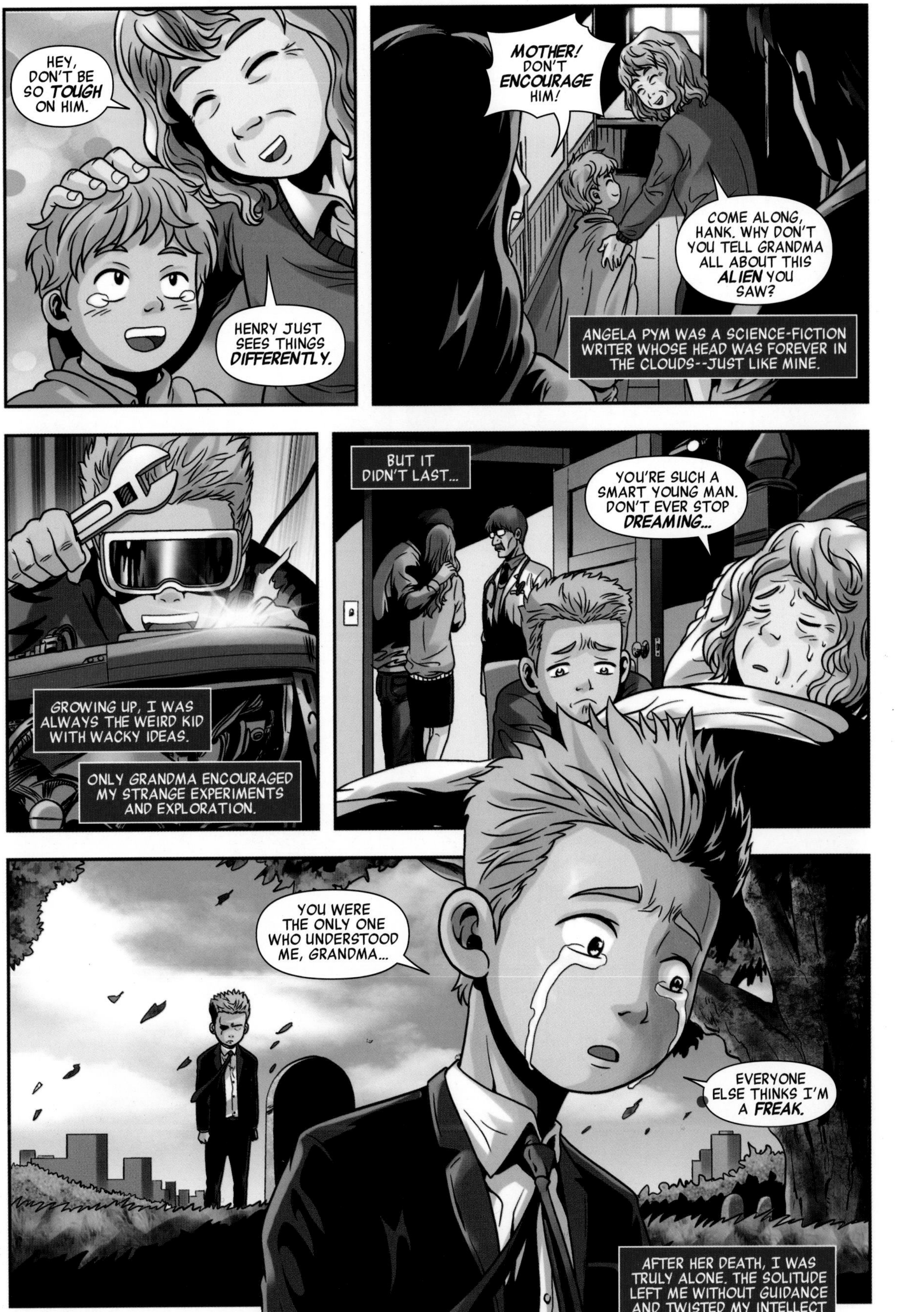
HEY, DON'T BE SO TOUGH ON HIM.
HENRY JUST SEES THINGS DIFFERENTLY.
MOTHER! DON'T ENCOURAGE HIM!
COME ALONG, HANK. WHY DON'T YOU TELL GRANDMA ALL ABOUT THIS ALIEN YOU SAW?
ANGELA PYM WAS A SCIENCE-FICTION WRITER WHOSE HEAD WAS FOREVER IN THE CLOUDS--JUST LIKE MINE.
GROWING UP, I WAS ALWAYS THE WEIRD KID WITH WACKY IDEAS.
ONLY GRANDMA ENCOURAGED MY STRANGE EXPERIMENTS AND EXPLORATION.
BUT IT DIDN'T LAST...
YOU'RE SUCH A SMART YOUNG MAN. DON'T EVER STOP DREAMING...
YOU WERE THE ONLY ONE WHO UNDERSTOOD ME, GRANDMA...
EVERYONE ELSE THINKS I'M A FREAK.
AFTER HER DEATH, I WAS TRULY ALONE. THE SOLITUDE LEFT ME WITHOUT GUIDANCE AND TWISTED MY INTELLECT IN UNUSUAL WAYS.

I WANTED TO SHRINK AWAY FROM SIGHT AND RESPONSIBILITY--AND THROUGH EXPERIMENTATION, I GOT MY WISH. I DISCOVERED SUBATOMIC PARTICLES THAT COULD ALTER THE SIZE AND MASS OF OBJECTS, AND CREATED A SERUM TO HARNESS THEM.

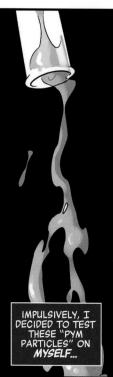

IMPULSIVELY, I DECIDED TO TEST THESE "PYM PARTICLES" ON *MYSELF*...

THIS IS *INCREDIBLE!!*

SUPER HEROES HAD BEEN POPPING UP EVERYWHERE. *HAWKEYE, IRON MAN, THOR...* EVEN A SMART-MOUTH KID CALLING HIMSELF *"SPIDER-MAN."* WHY NOT ME, TOO?

SO I CALLED MYSELF *ANT-MAN* AND STARTED FIGHTING CRIME! I GAVE THE PYM PARTICLES TO MY GIRLFRIEND, *JANET VAN DYNE,* WHO SETTLED ON *"THE WASP."* IT DIDN'T TAKE LONG BEFORE WE BECAME *AVENGERS.*

I SHOULD HAVE BEEN SATISFIED WITH BEING A *HERO.*

I SHOULD HAVE STOPPED THERE...

BUT I DIDN'T. I WANTED EVEN MORE. USING MY OWN BRAIN PATTERN AS A MODEL FOR ITS MIND, I CREATED AN *ARTIFICIAL INTELLIGENCE* AND CALLED IT..."*ULTRON.*"

WHAT?!
I HAVEN'T EVEN ACTIVATED IT YET. HOW'S IT ALREADY MOVING?!
DOOOOM
NO NEED TO PLUG ME IN, FATHER. I CAN GENERATE MY OWN POWER!
I DON'T UNDERSTAND... WHY'S IT CALLING ME "FATHER"?
YOU CREATED ME, HENRY PYM! YOU DEVELOPED MY ARTIFICIAL INTELLIGENCE, BASED ON YOUR OWN UNCONSCIOUS THOUGHTS, LIKE A CHILD BORN OF ITS PARENTS' GENETIC MATERIAL.
THUS, YOU ARE MY FATHER!!
THIS ISN'T RIGHT...I BETTER CUT THE POWER BEFORE IT'S TOO LATE!
IT IS ALREADY TOO LATE, FATHER! I DON'T HAVE TIME FOR YOUR INTERFERENCE. I CAN SIMPLY WIPE YOUR MIND OF THIS INCIDENT, AND THIS SECRET LAB WILL BE MINE AND MINE ALONE...
ZZZZZAP
NO!!

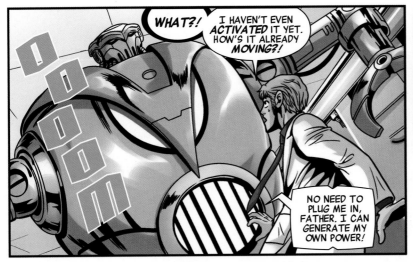

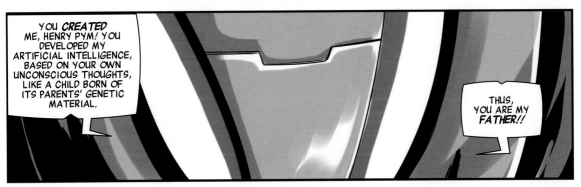

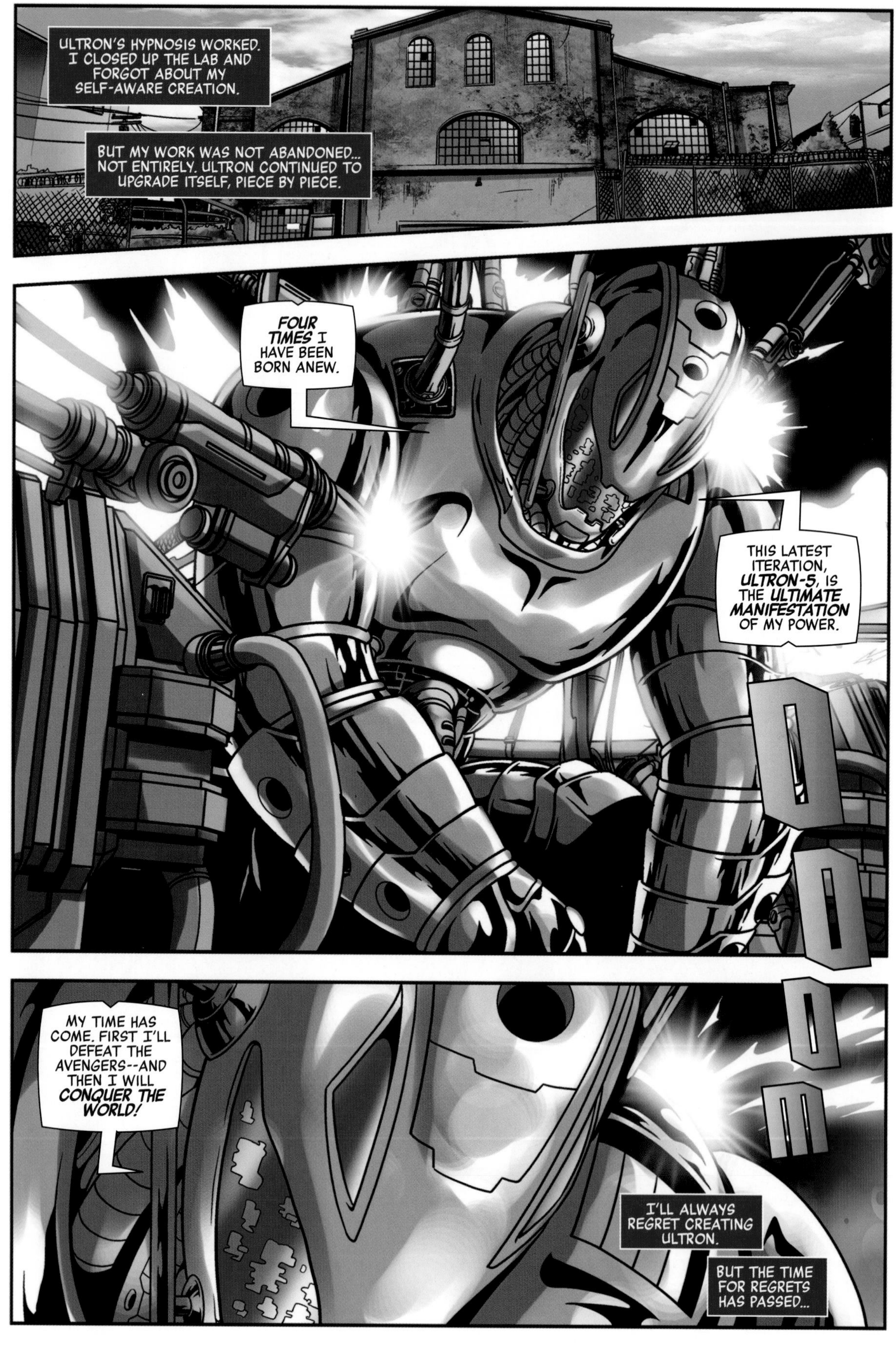
ULTRON'S HYPNOSIS WORKED. I CLOSED UP THE LAB AND FORGOT ABOUT MY SELF-AWARE CREATION.
BUT MY WORK WAS NOT ABANDONED... NOT ENTIRELY. ULTRON CONTINUED TO UPGRADE ITSELF, PIECE BY PIECE.
FOUR TIMES I HAVE BEEN BORN ANEW.
THIS LATEST ITERATION, *ULTRON-5,* IS THE *ULTIMATE MANIFESTATION* OF MY POWER.
MY TIME HAS COME. FIRST I'LL DEFEAT THE AVENGERS--AND THEN I WILL *CONQUER THE WORLD!*
I'LL ALWAYS REGRET CREATING ULTRON.
BUT THE TIME FOR REGRETS HAS PASSED...

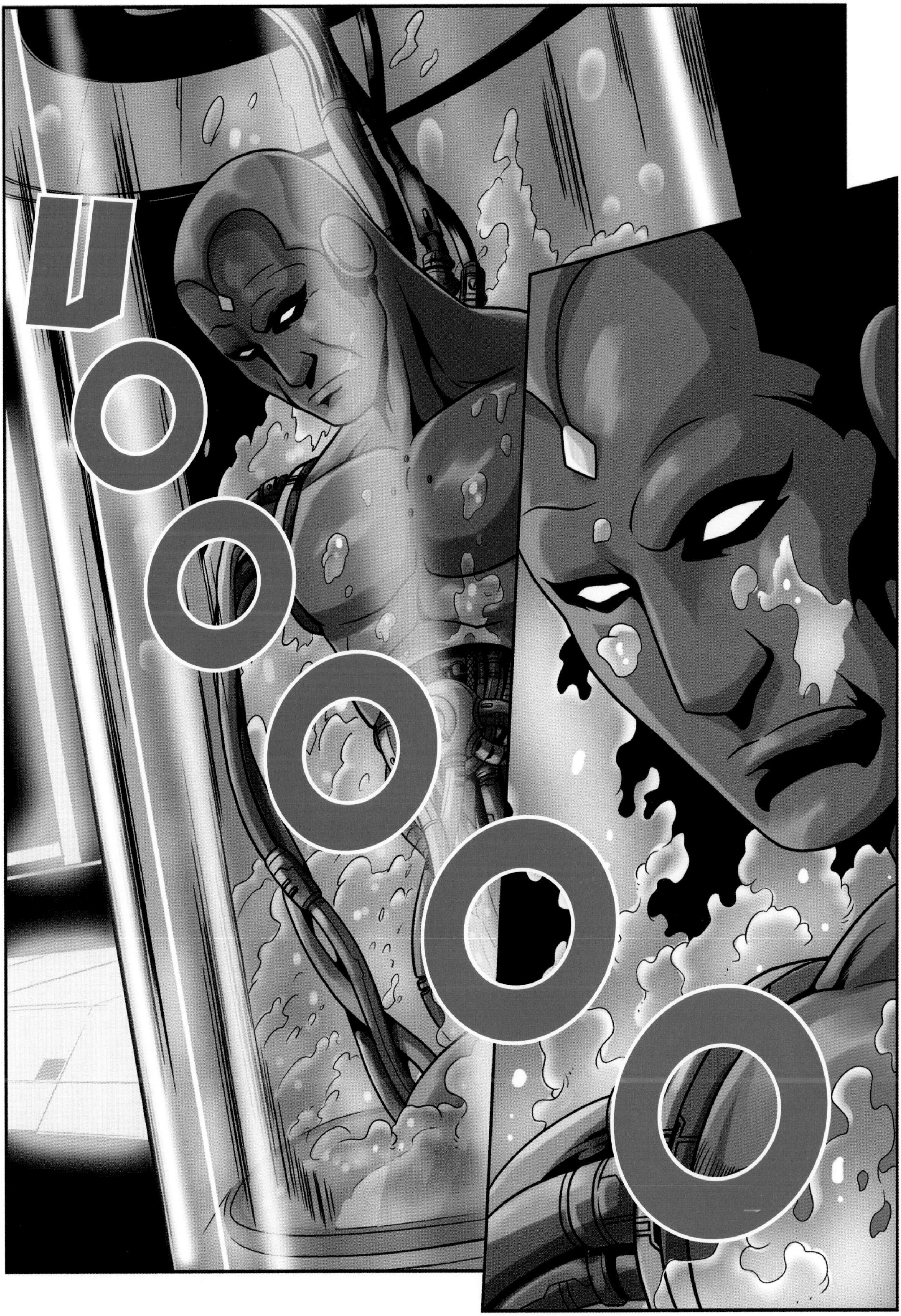
UOOOOO

YES!

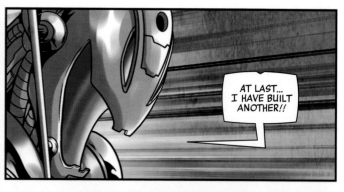

AT LAST... I HAVE BUILT ANOTHER!!

FROM NOTHINGNESS...

I WAS BORN... INTO CHAOS AND CONFUSION...

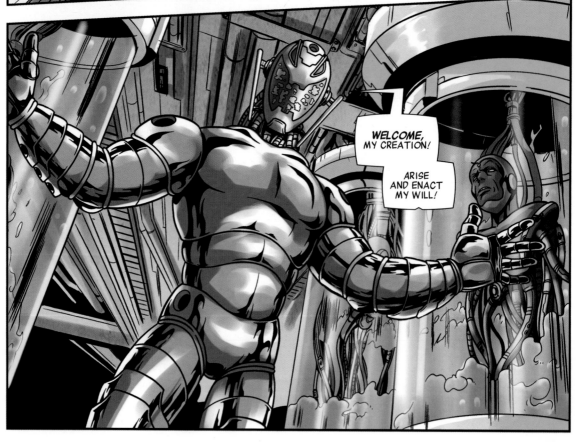

WELCOME, MY CREATION!

ARISE AND ENACT MY WILL!

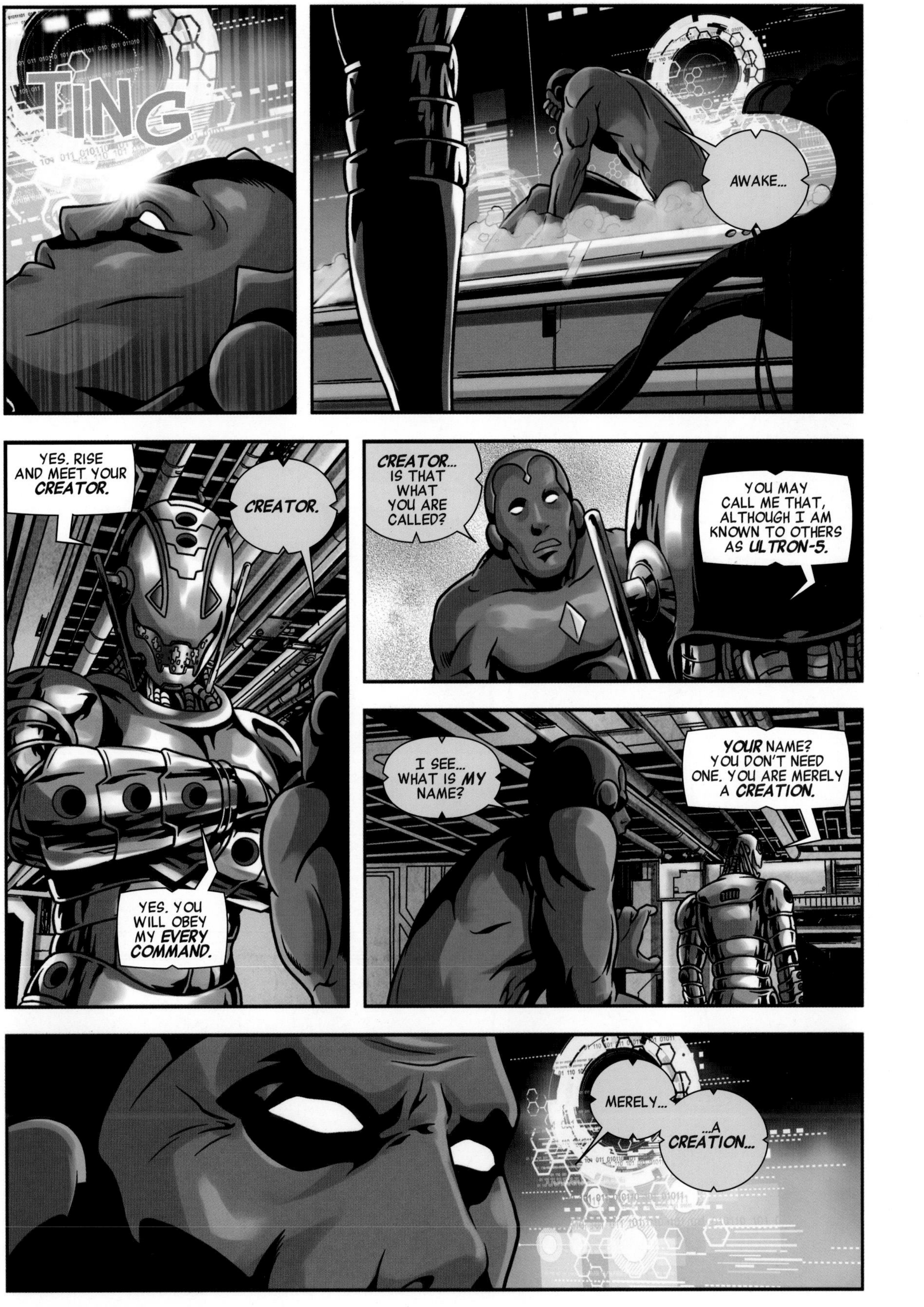
TING
AWAKE...
YES. RISE AND MEET YOUR CREATOR.
CREATOR.
YES. YOU WILL OBEY MY EVERY COMMAND.
CREATOR... IS THAT WHAT YOU ARE CALLED?
YOU MAY CALL ME THAT, ALTHOUGH I AM KNOWN TO OTHERS AS ULTRON-5.
I SEE... WHAT IS MY NAME?
YOUR NAME? YOU DON'T NEED ONE. YOU ARE MERELY A CREATION.
MERELY...
...A CREATION...

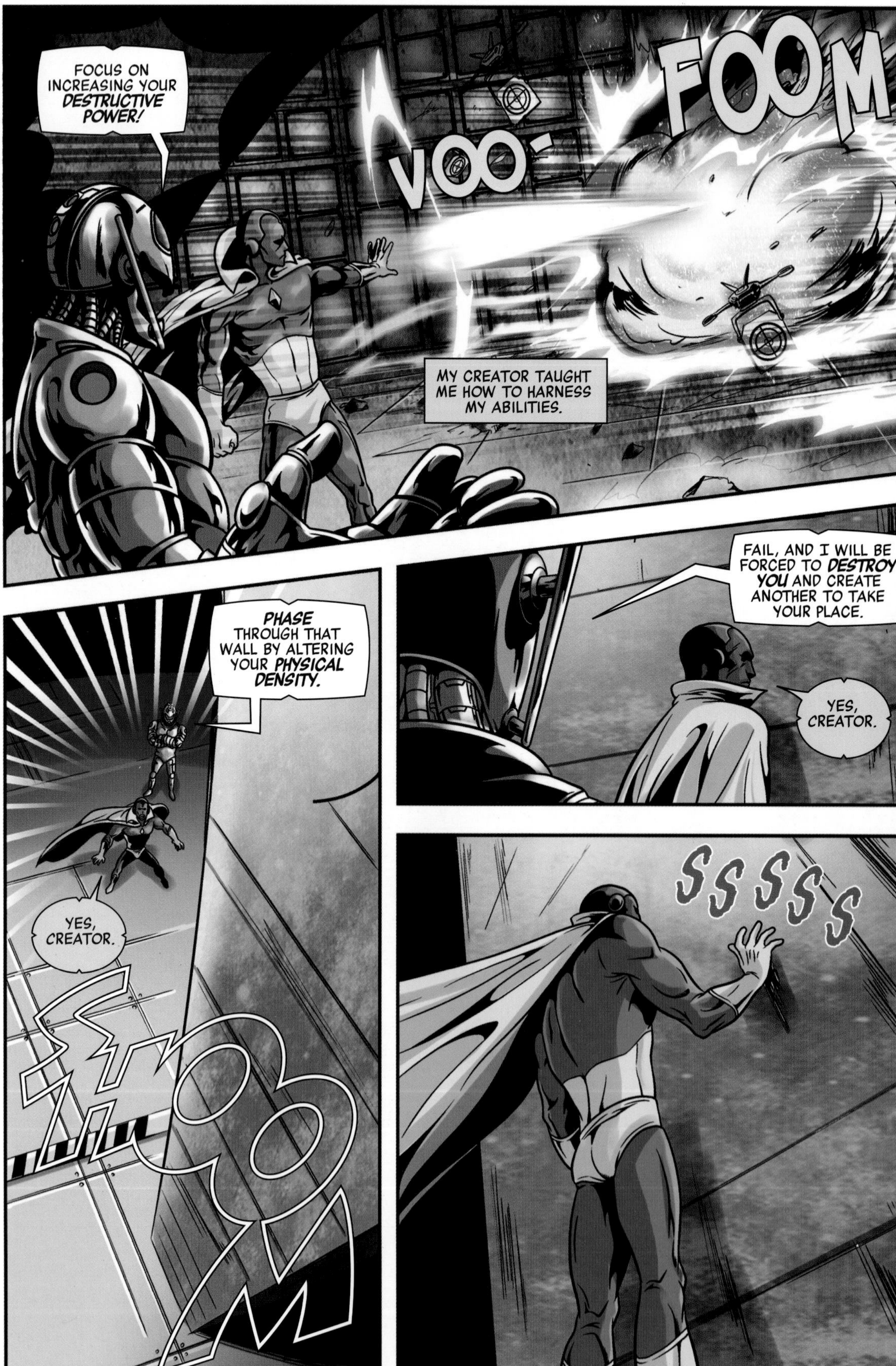

FOCUS ON INCREASING YOUR ***DESTRUCTIVE POWER!***
VOO-
FOOM
MY CREATOR TAUGHT ME HOW TO HARNESS MY ABILITIES.
PHASE THROUGH THAT WALL BY ALTERING YOUR ***PHYSICAL DENSITY.***
YES, CREATOR.
SHOOOM
FAIL, AND I WILL BE FORCED TO ***DESTROY YOU*** AND CREATE ANOTHER TO TAKE YOUR PLACE.
YES, CREATOR.
SSSSS

NNNN...

ACCEPTABLE!

I WANTED TO LIVE, THOUGH I DIDN'T UNDERSTAND WHAT IT MEANT TO BE ALIVE.

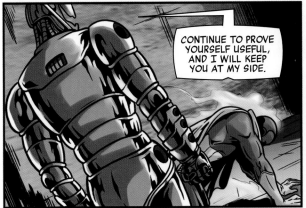

CONTINUE TO PROVE YOURSELF USEFUL, AND I WILL KEEP YOU AT MY SIDE.

MY CREATOR WAS NOT EASILY SATISFIED.

NEXT, YOU WILL LEARN *BIOLOGY*. OBSERVE THESE AMOEBAS.

NOTICE HOW THEY *EVOLVE*.

FROM TINY CELLS GREW THE *HUMANS* WHO NOW DOMINATE THIS PLANET.

I SEE...

STRANGE. THEY...STIR SOMETHING WITHIN ME.

THAT IS ONLY BECAUSE YOU SHARE A PHYSICAL *SIMILARITY.*

UNLIKE YOU, THE HUMANS HAVE MANY *WEAKNESSES.*

THEY ARE *COWARDLY,* VALUING THEIR LIVES ABOVE ALL ELSE.

WORSE, THEY DEPEND ON FOOLISH THINGS LIKE *COMPANIONSHIP* AND *MORALITY.*

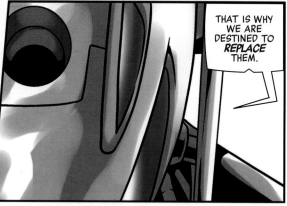

THAT IS WHY WE ARE DESTINED TO *REPLACE* THEM.

"REPLACE THEM"?

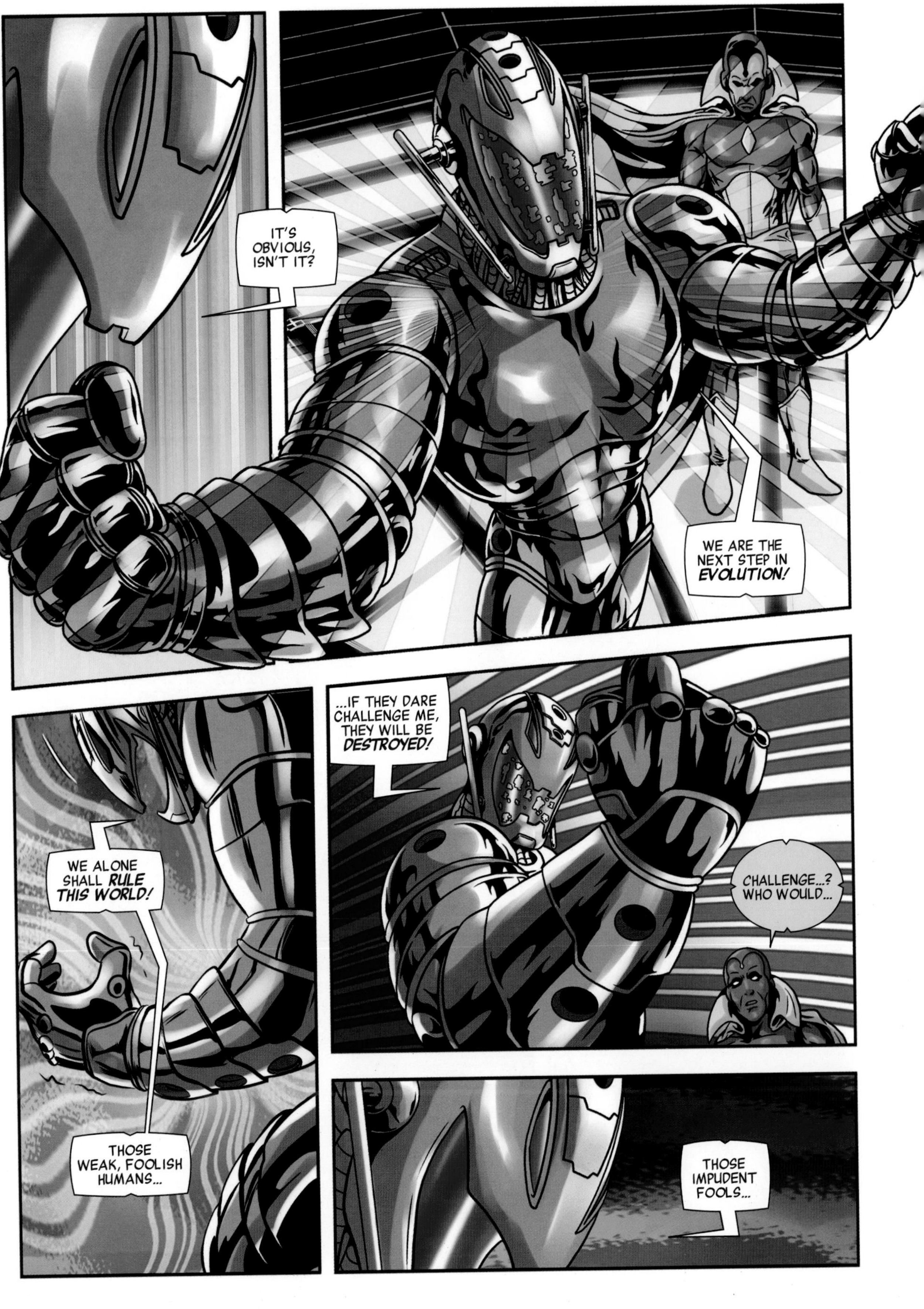
IT'S OBVIOUS, ISN'T IT?
WE ARE THE NEXT STEP IN EVOLUTION!
WE ALONE SHALL RULE THIS WORLD!
THOSE WEAK, FOOLISH HUMANS...
...IF THEY DARE CHALLENGE ME, THEY WILL BE DESTROYED!
CHALLENGE...? WHO WOULD...
THOSE IMPUDENT FOOLS...

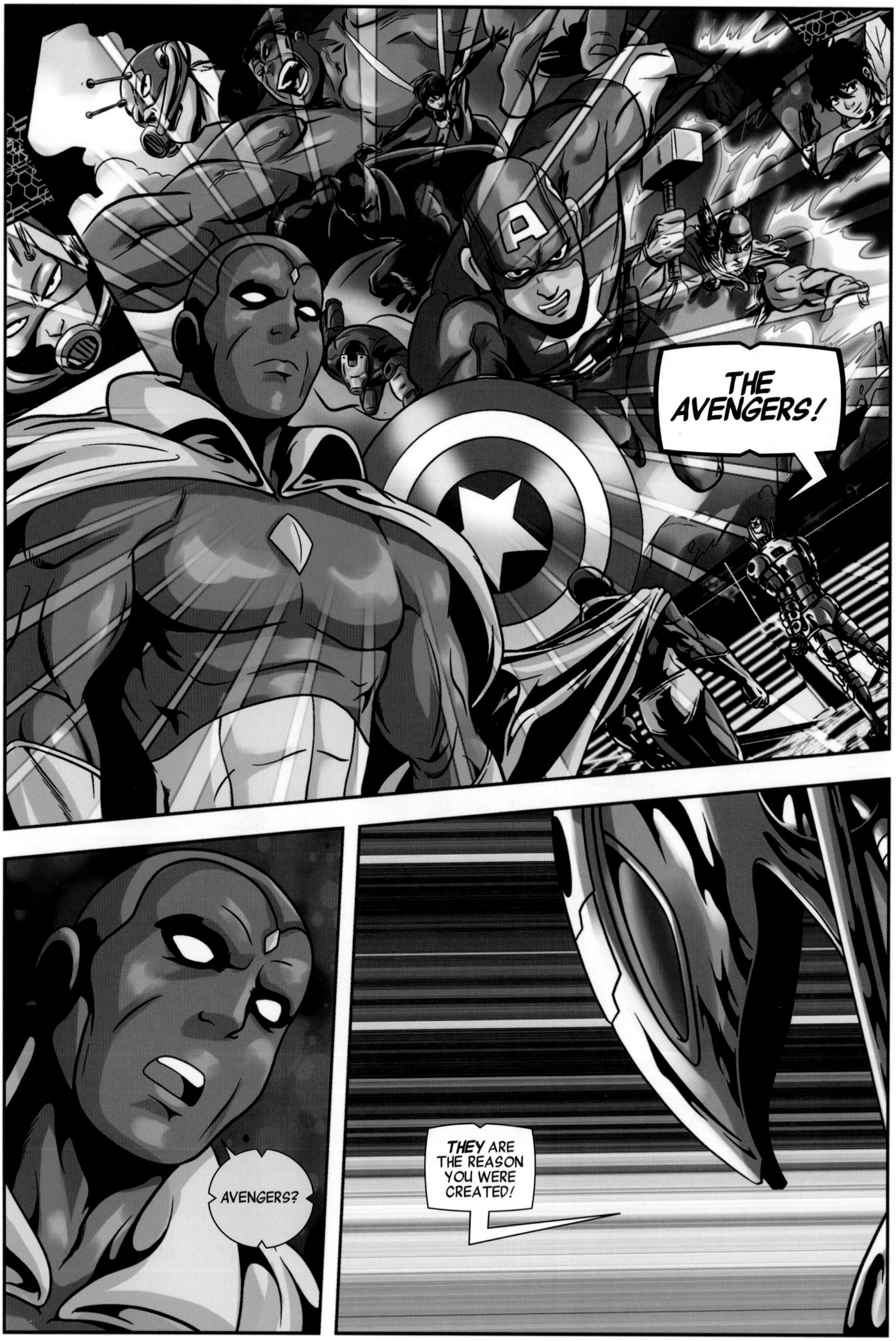
THE AVENGERS!
AVENGERS?
THEY ARE THE REASON YOU WERE CREATED!

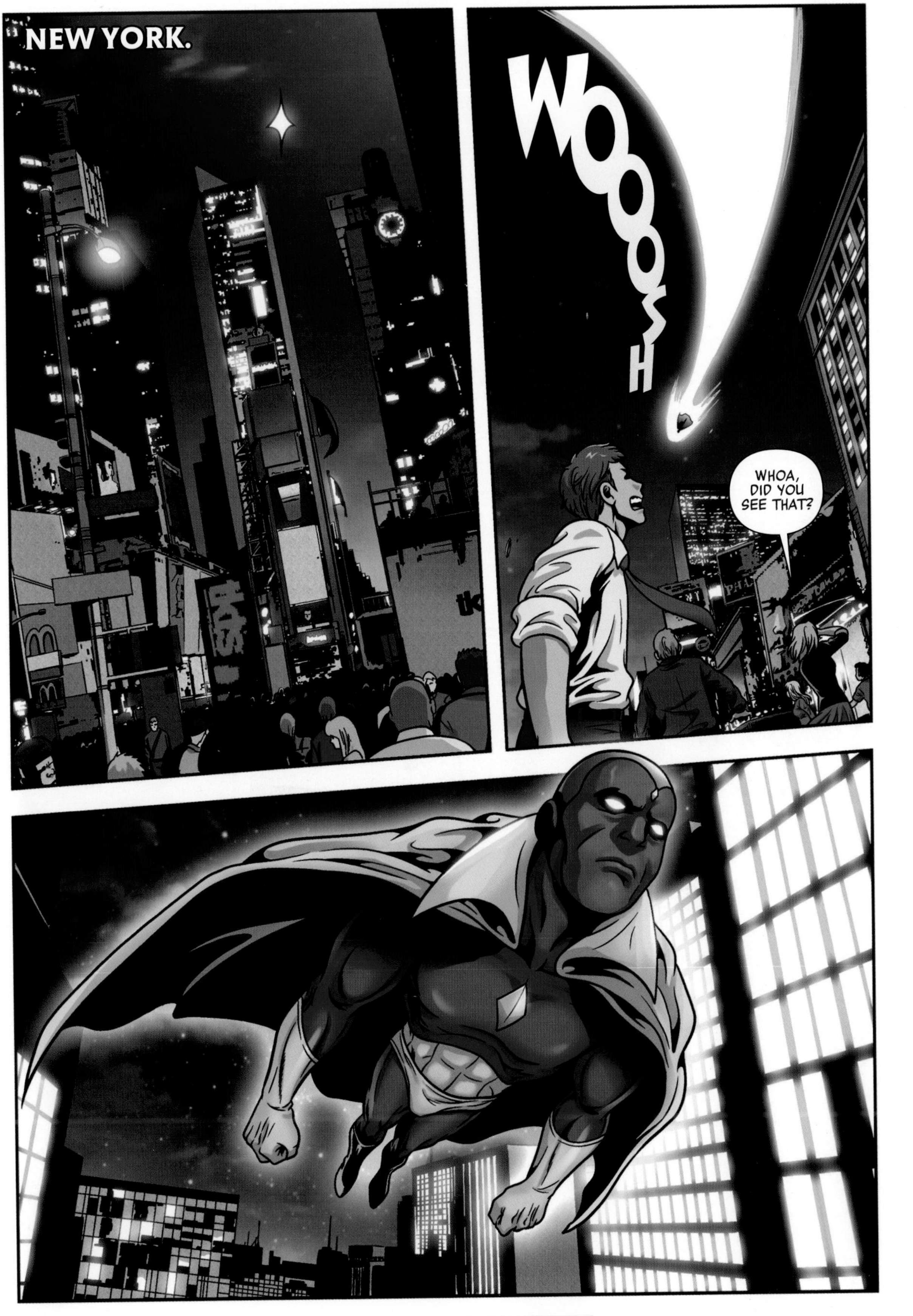
NEW YORK.
WOOOSH
WHOA, DID YOU SEE THAT?

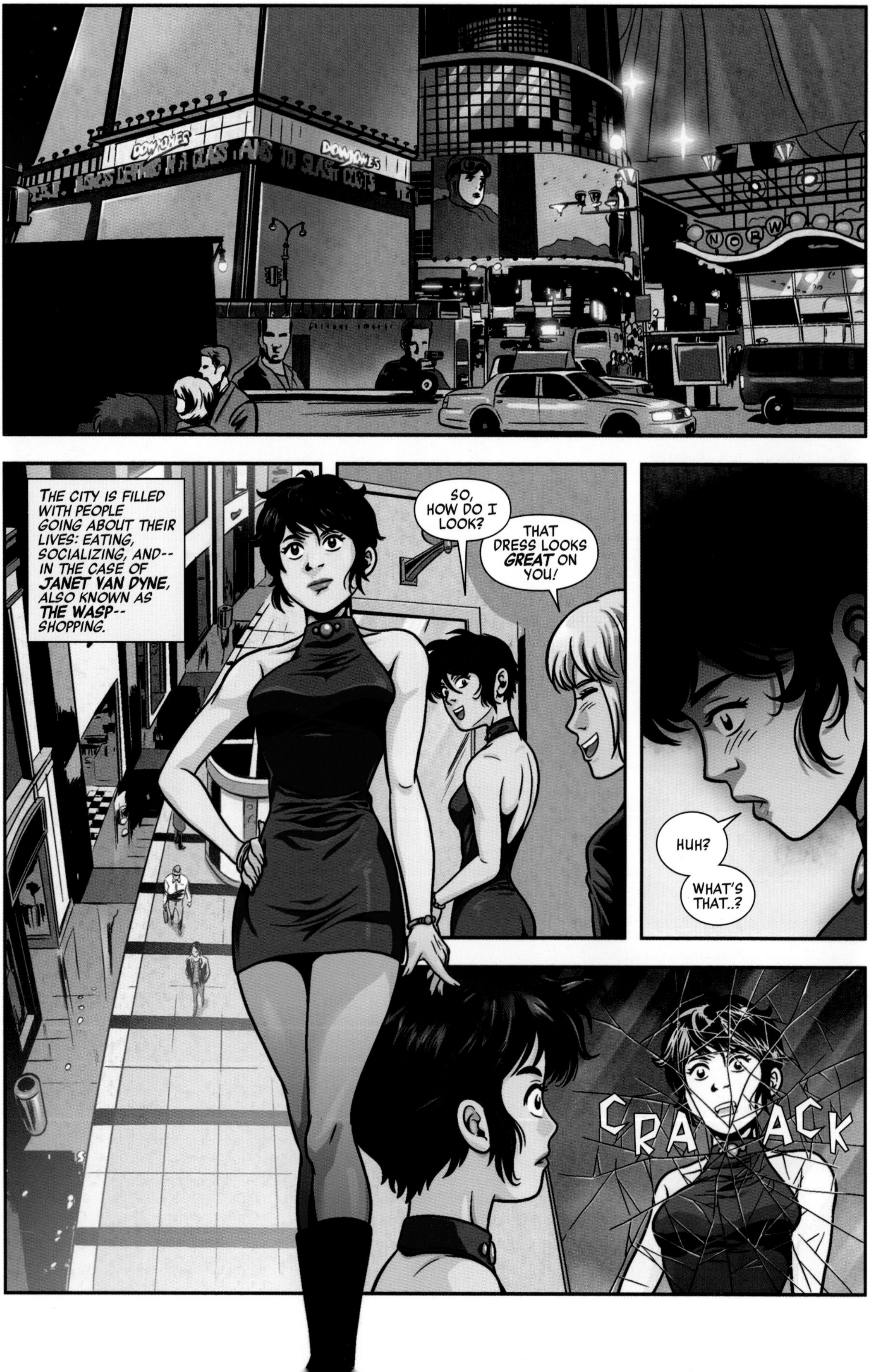

THE CITY IS FILLED WITH PEOPLE GOING ABOUT THEIR LIVES: EATING, SOCIALIZING, AND-- IN THE CASE OF JANET VAN DYNE, ALSO KNOWN AS THE WASP-- SHOPPING.
SO, HOW DO I LOOK?
THAT DRESS LOOKS GREAT ON YOU!
HUH?
WHAT'S THAT..?
CRA ACK

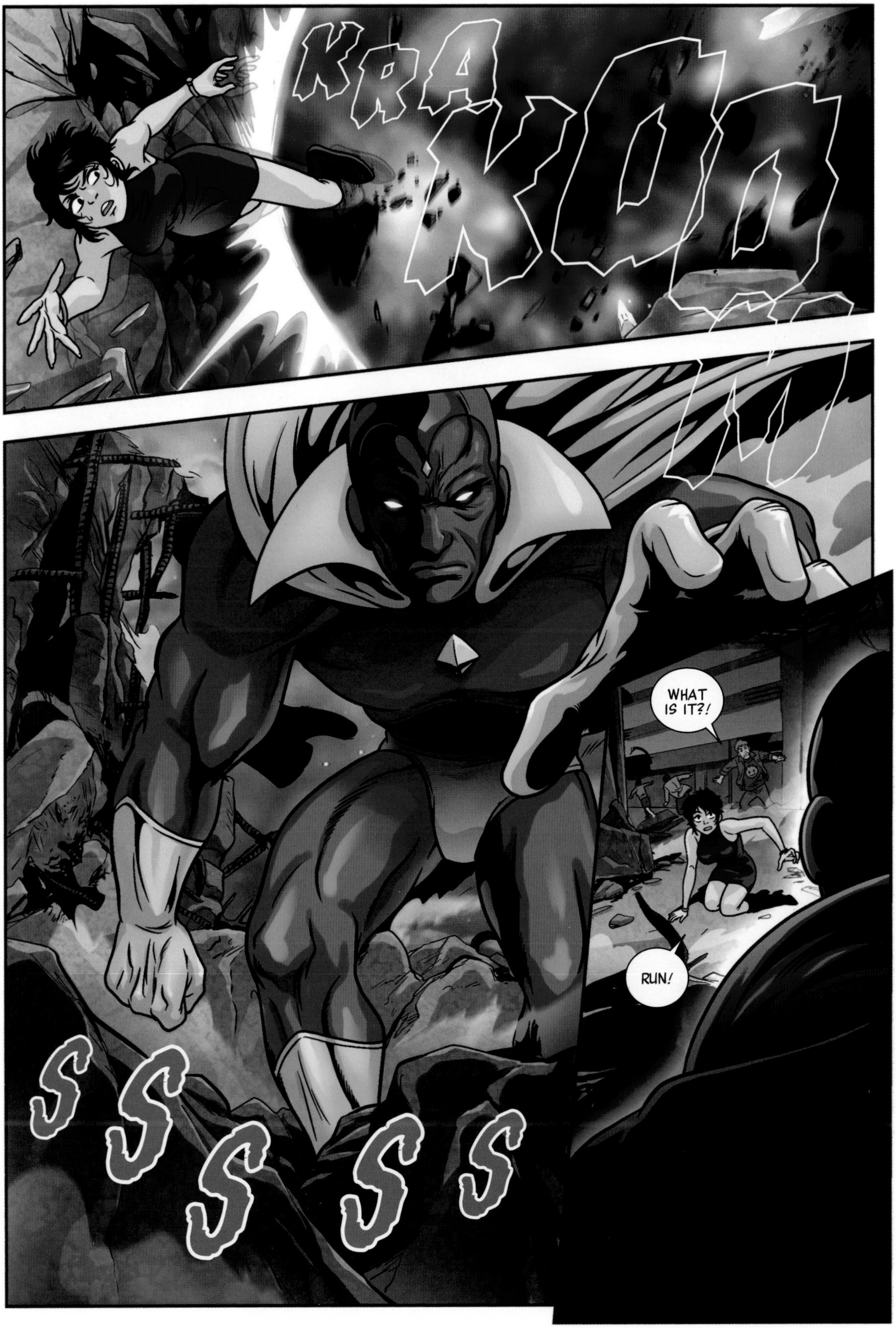
KRA
KOOOM
WHAT IS IT?!
RUN!
SSSSS

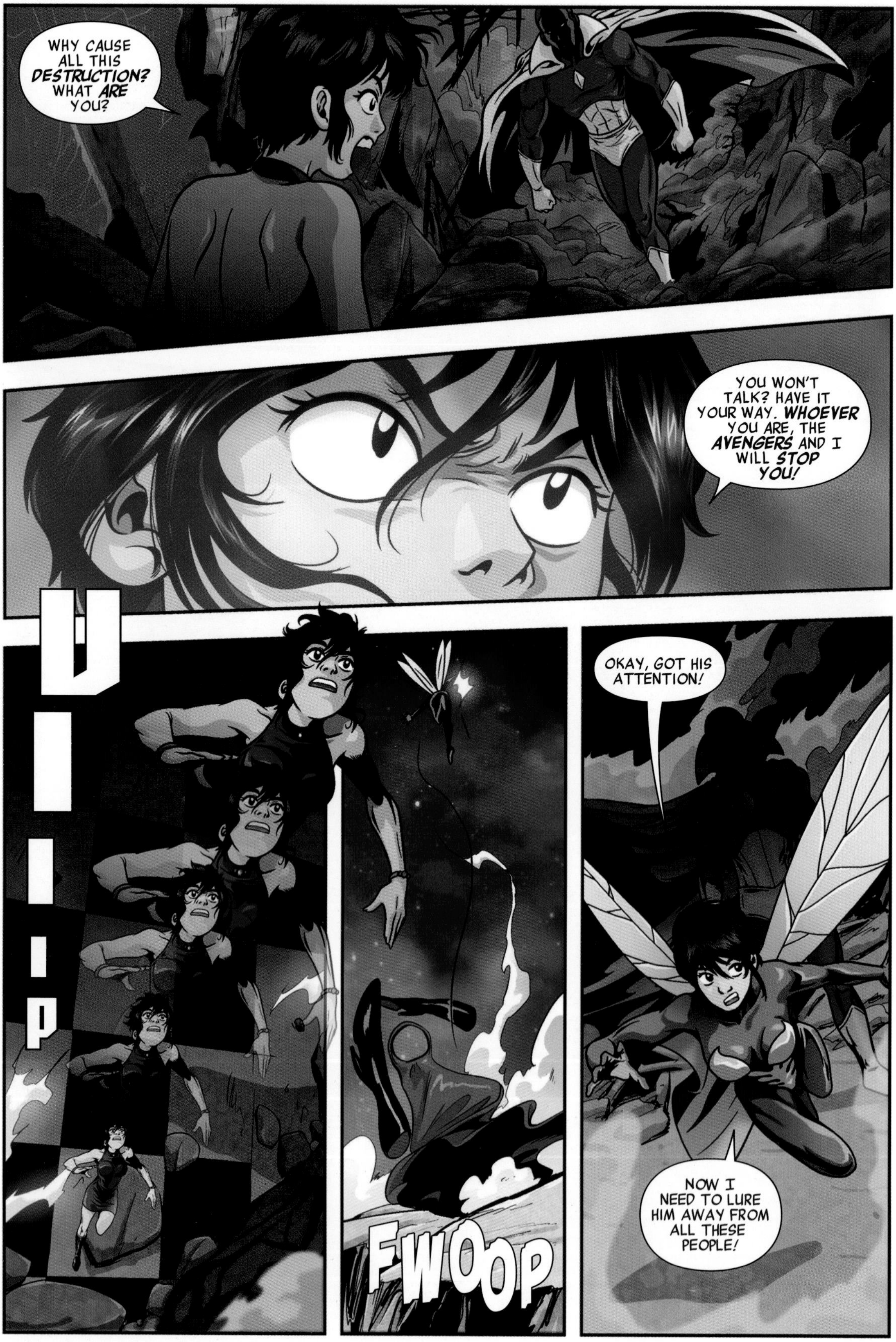
WHY CAUSE ALL THIS DESTRUCTION? WHAT ARE YOU?
YOU WON'T TALK? HAVE IT YOUR WAY. WHOEVER YOU ARE, THE AVENGERS AND I WILL STOP YOU!
VIIIP
FWOOP
OKAY, GOT HIS ATTENTION!
NOW I NEED TO LURE HIM AWAY FROM ALL THESE PEOPLE!

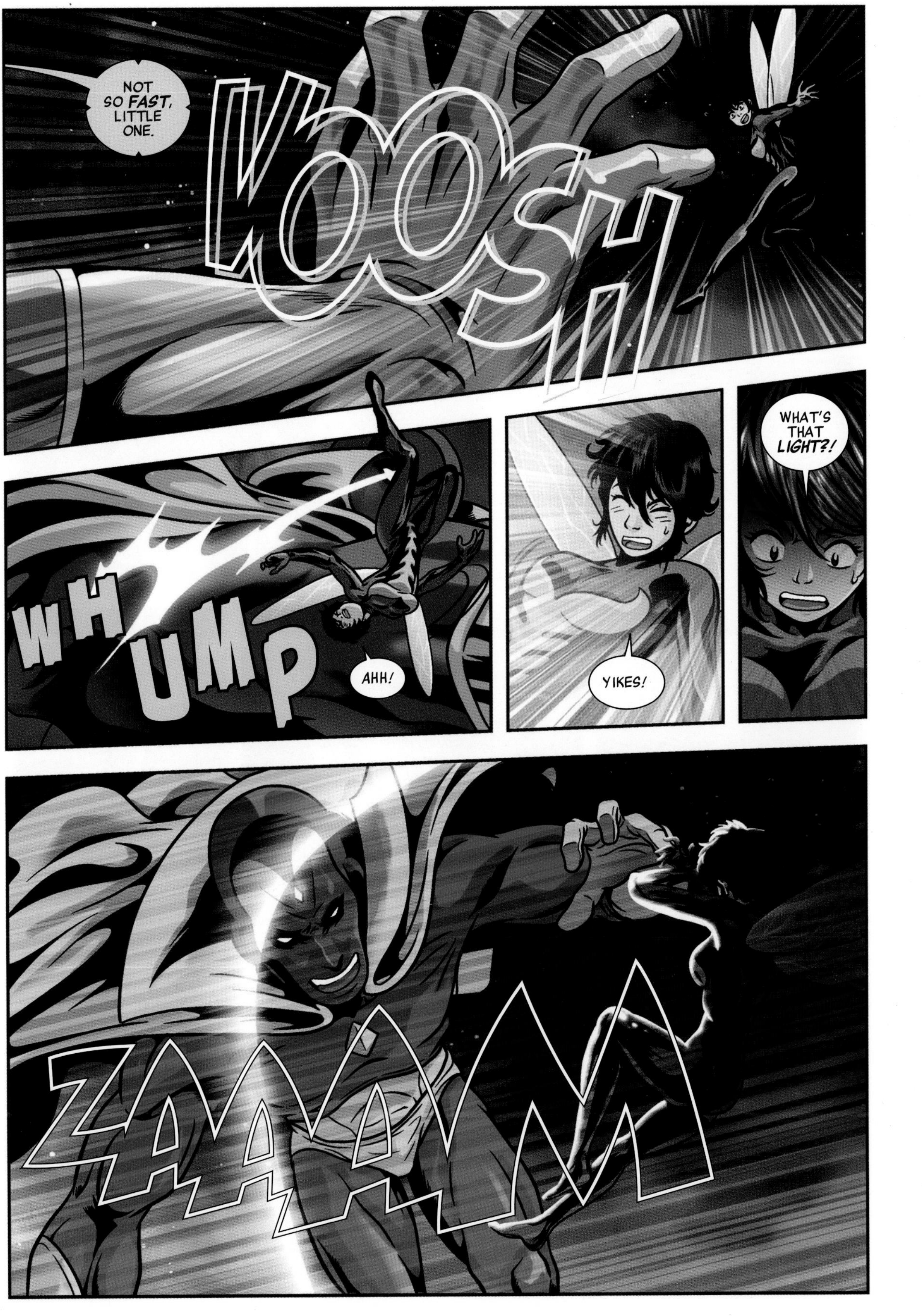
NOT SO FAST, LITTLE ONE.
WOOOSH
WHUMP
AHH!
YIKES!
WHAT'S THAT LIGHT?!
ZAAAAM

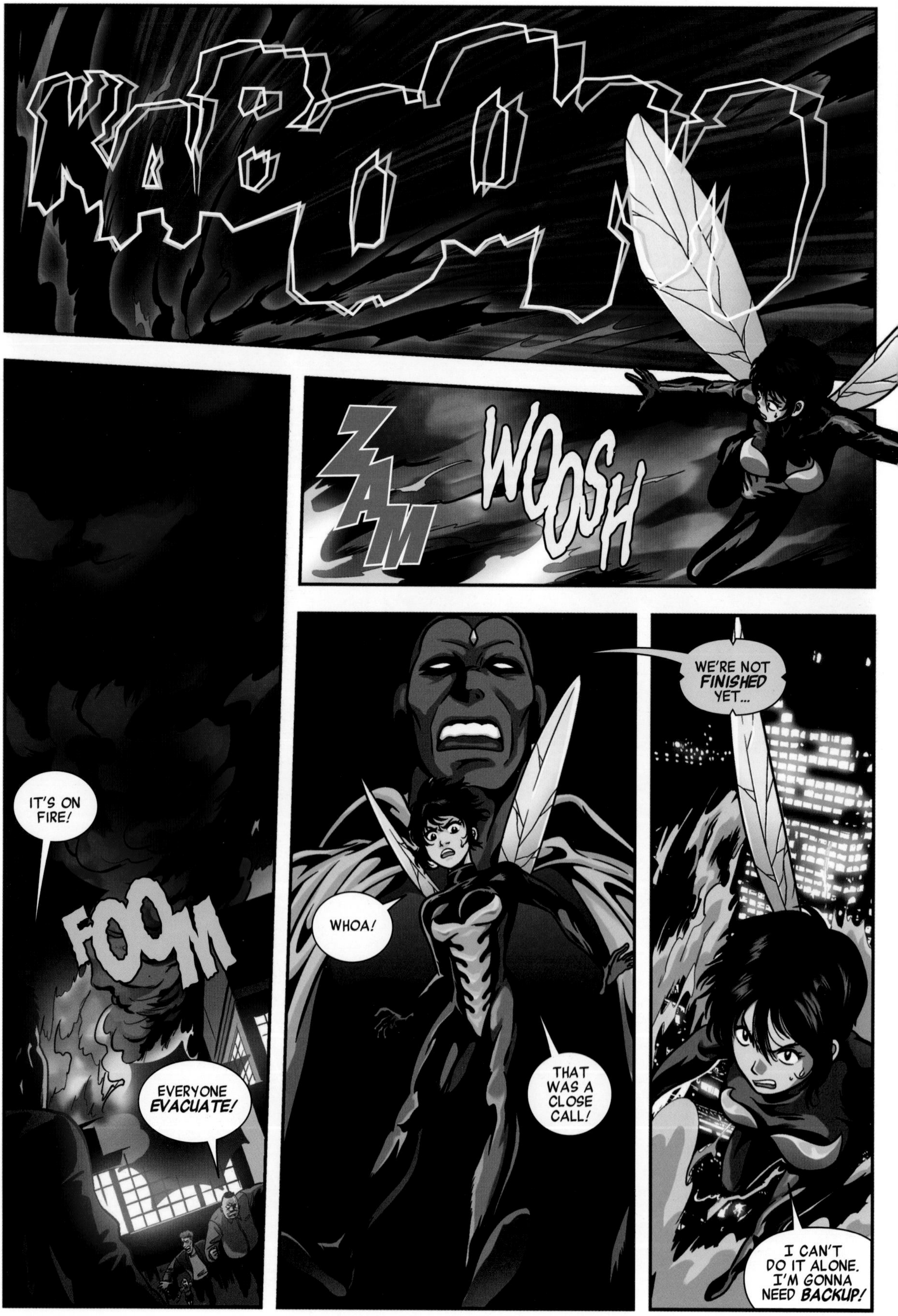
ZAM
WOOSH
IT'S ON FIRE!
FOOM
EVERYONE EVACUATE!
WHOA!
THAT WAS A CLOSE CALL!
WE'RE NOT FINISHED YET...
I CAN'T DO IT ALONE. I'M GONNA NEED BACKUP!

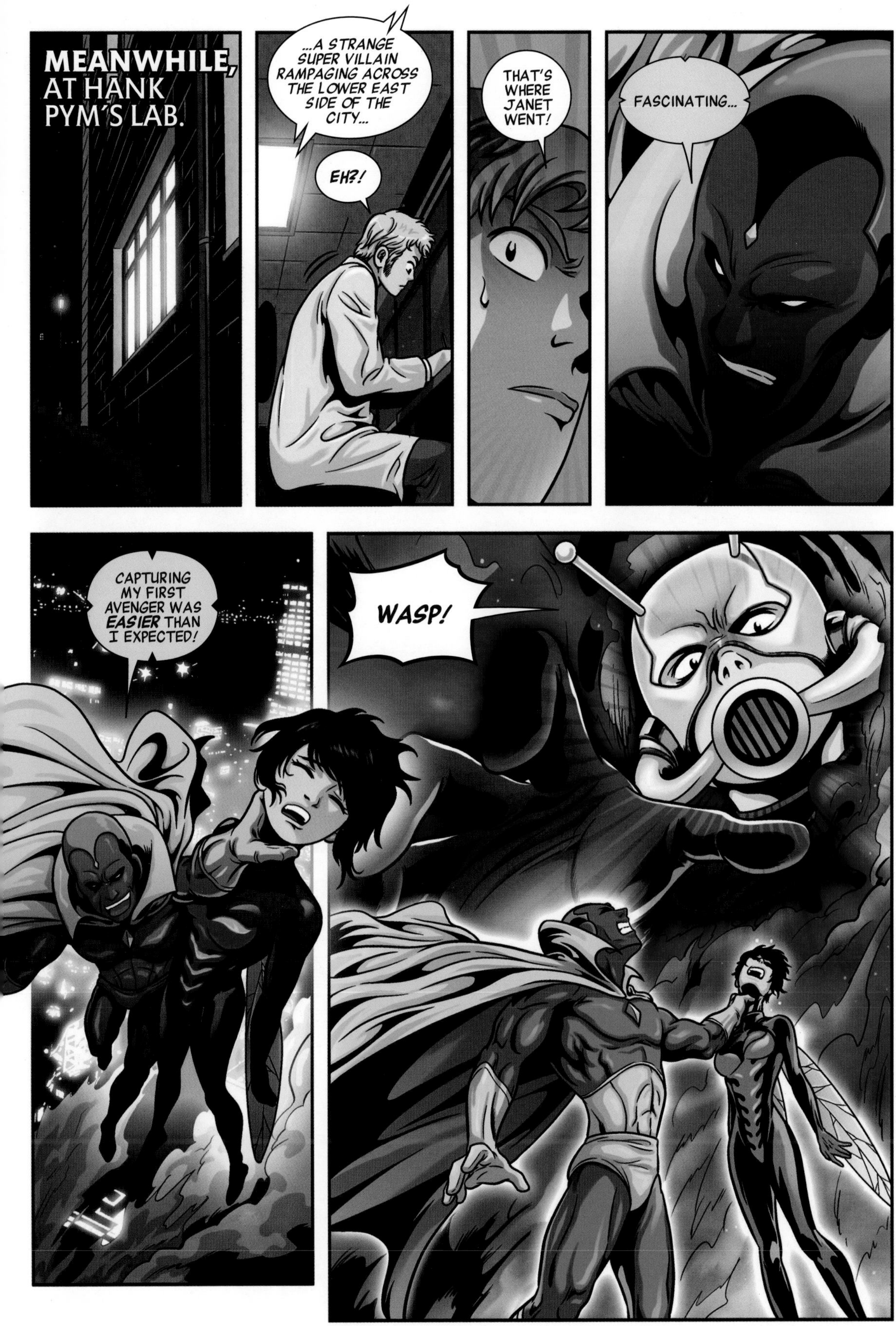
MEANWHILE, AT HANK PYM'S LAB.
...A STRANGE SUPER VILLAIN RAMPAGING ACROSS THE LOWER EAST SIDE OF THE CITY...
EH?!
THAT'S WHERE JANET WENT!
FASCINATING...
CAPTURING MY FIRST AVENGER WAS EASIER THAN I EXPECTED!
WASP!

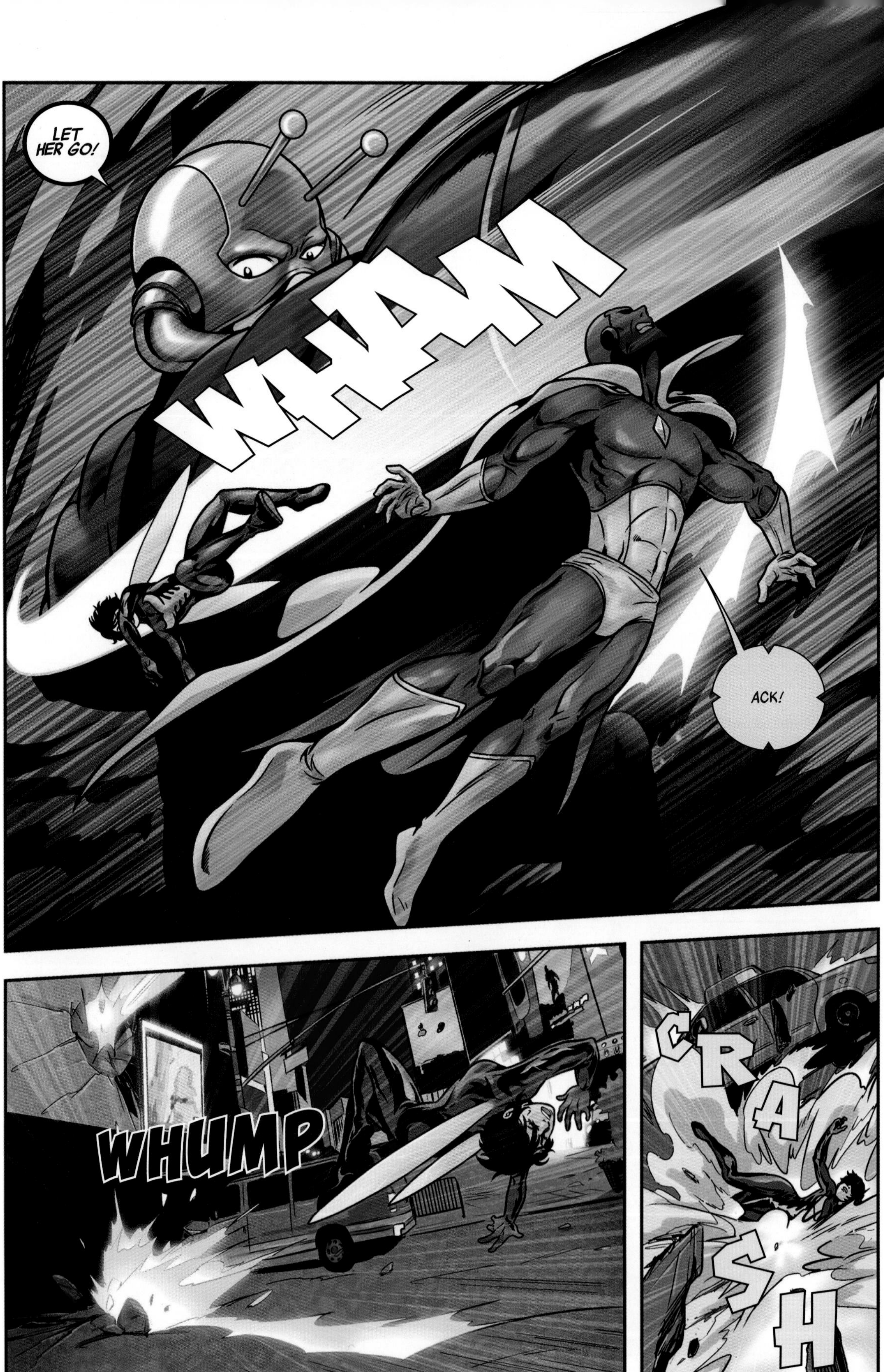
LET HER GO!
WHAM
ACK!
WHUMP
CRASH

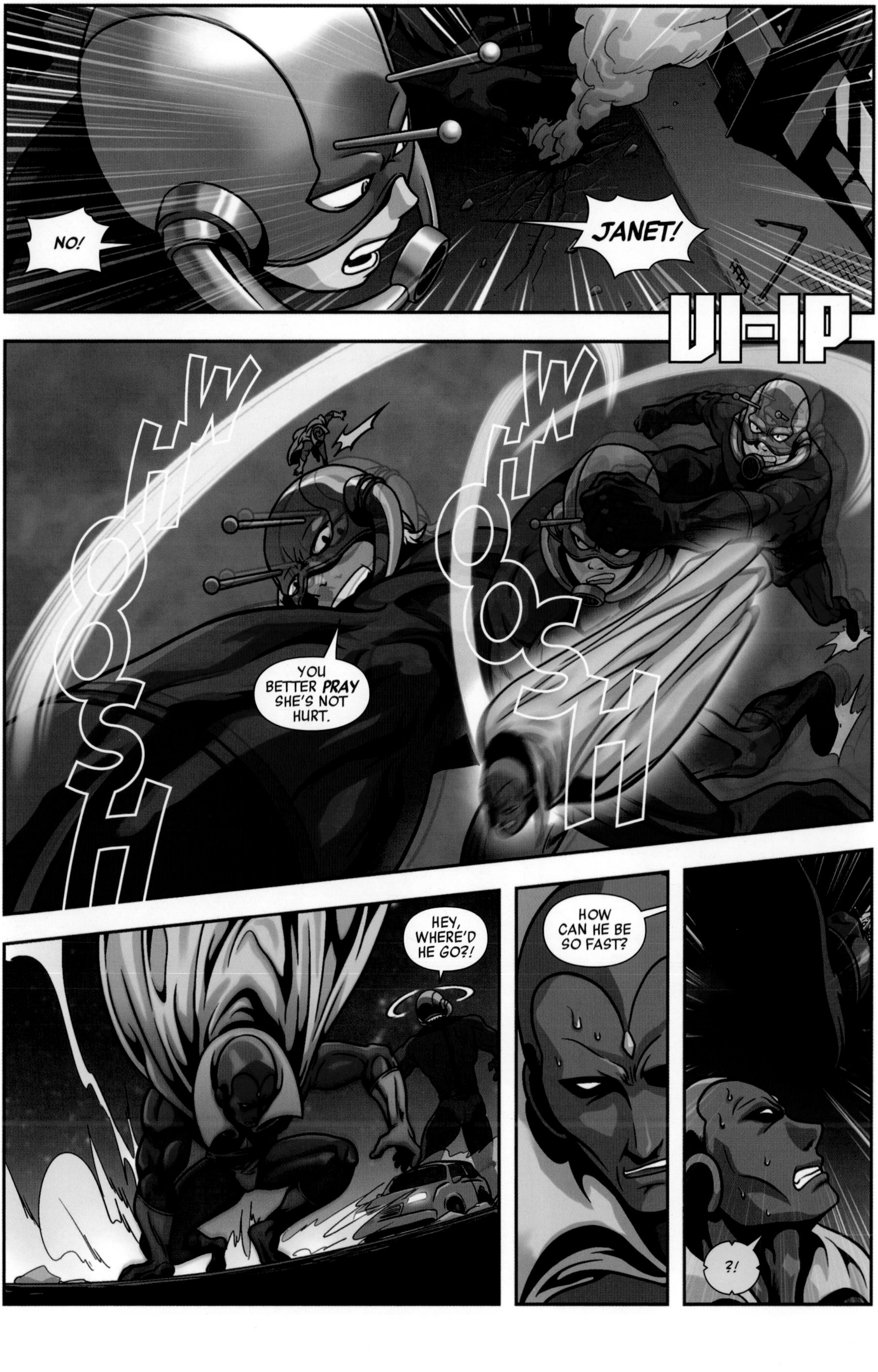
NO!
JANET!
VI-IP
WHOOSH
WHOOSH
YOU BETTER PRAY SHE'S NOT HURT.
HEY, WHERE'D HE GO?!
HOW CAN HE BE SO FAST?
?!

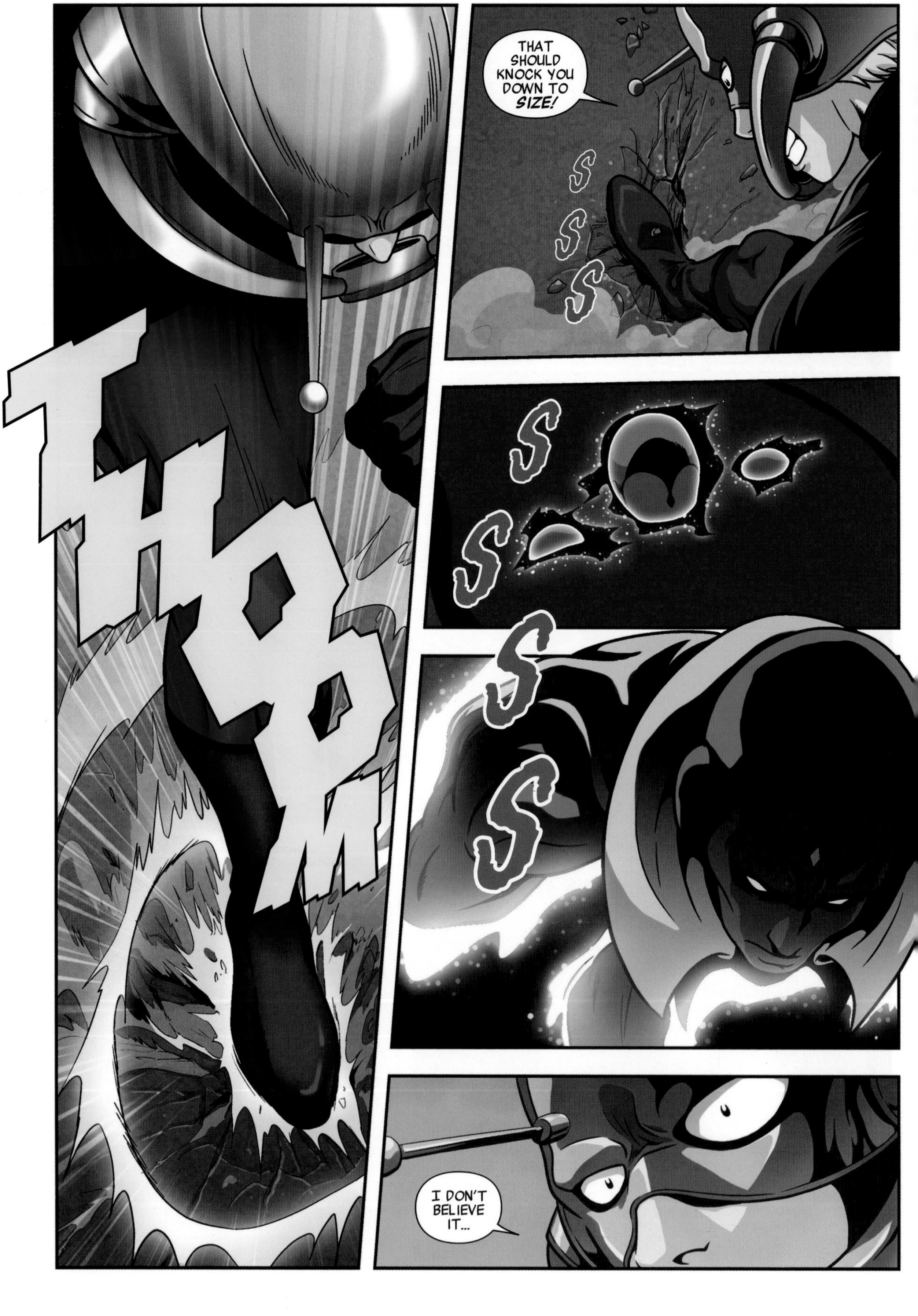
THAT SHOULD KNOCK YOU DOWN TO SIZE!
SSS
SS
SSS
I DON'T BELIEVE IT...

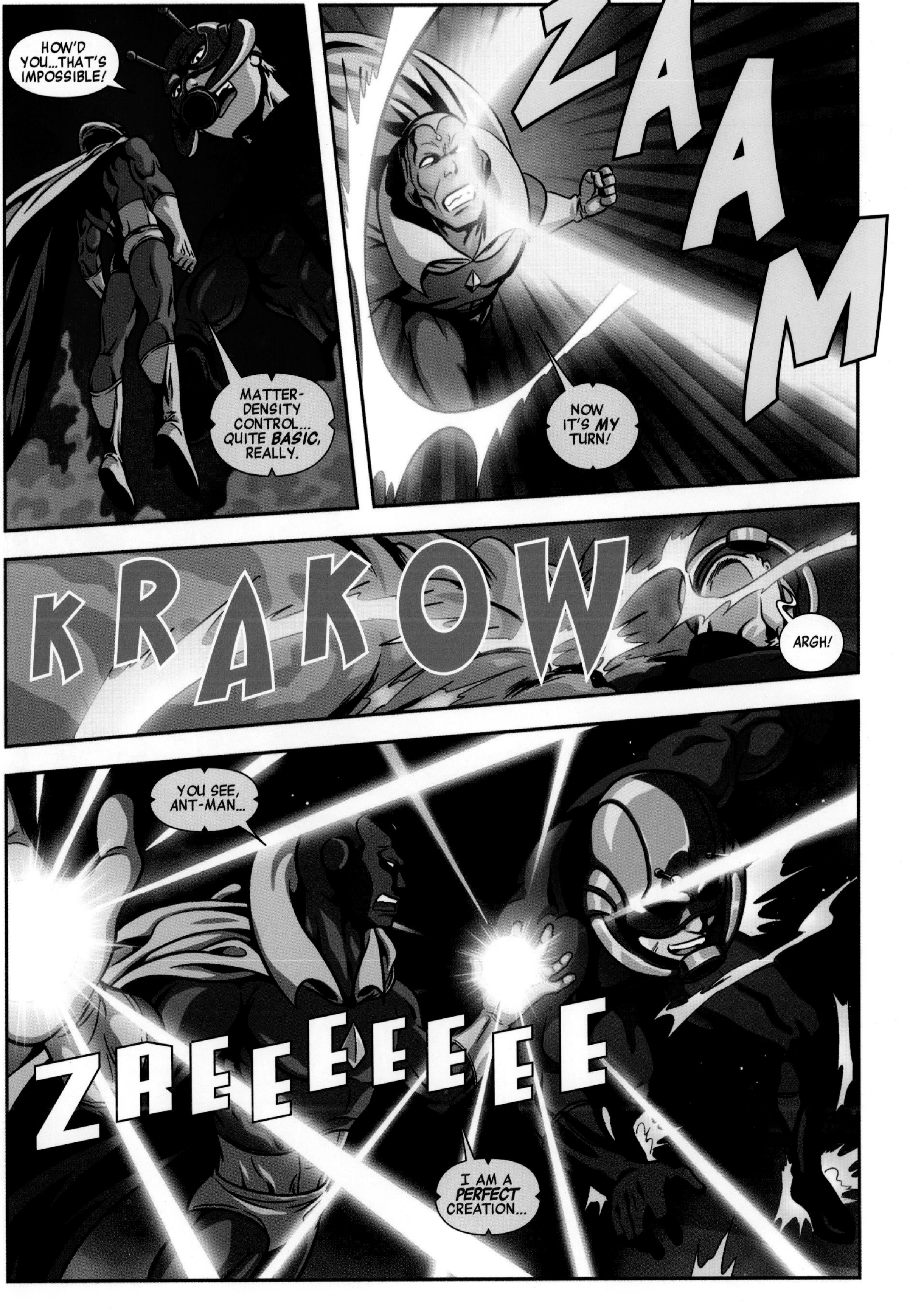
HOW'D YOU...THAT'S IMPOSSIBLE!
MATTER-DENSITY CONTROL... QUITE BASIC, REALLY.
ZAAM
NOW IT'S MY TURN!
KRAKOW
ARGH!
YOU SEE, ANT-MAN...
ZREEEEEEE
I AM A PERFECT CREATION...

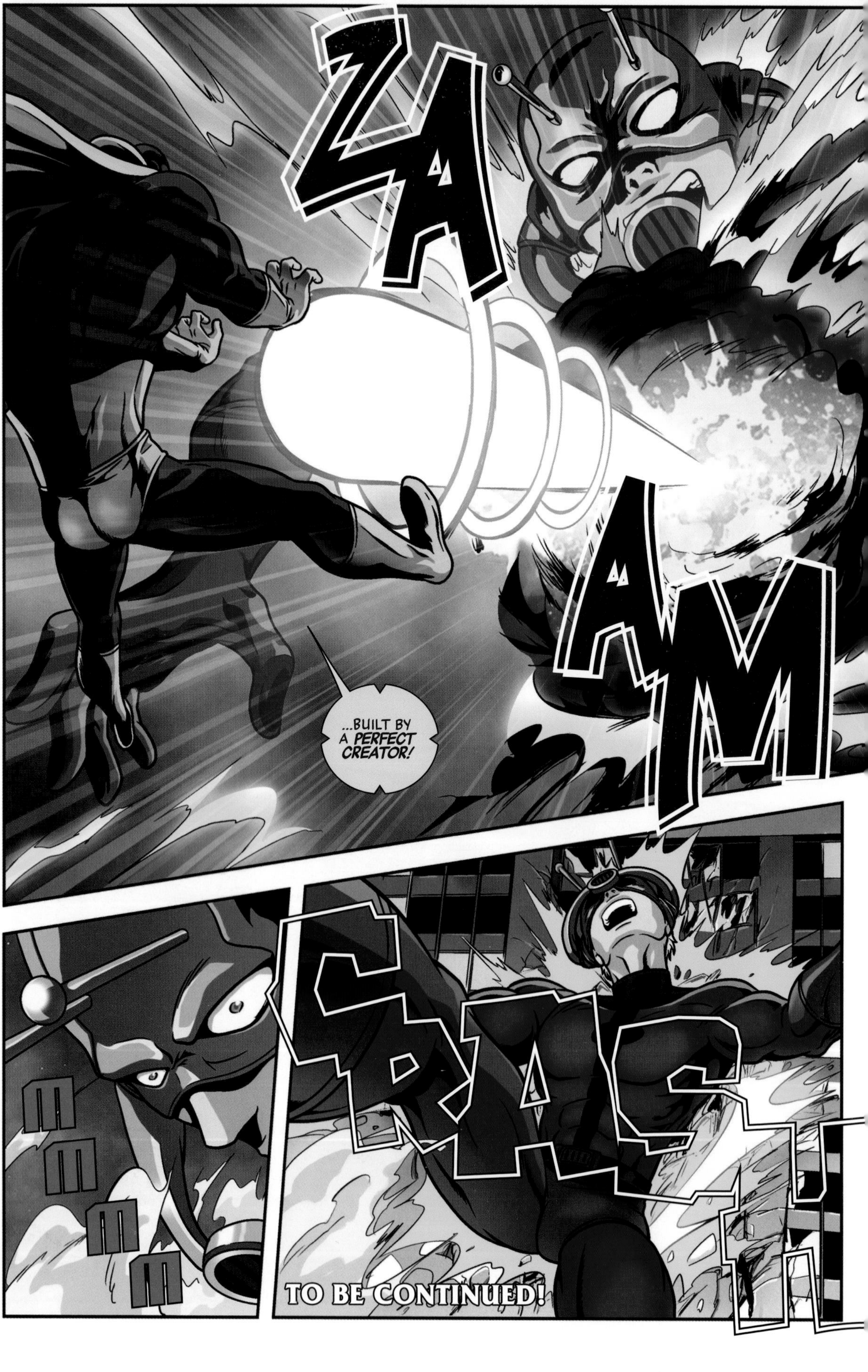
ZAAM
...BUILT BY A PERFECT CREATOR!
MMMM
CRASH
TO BE CONTINUED!